Artlist Collection
THE DOG

IS A PAW A FOOT?

All About Measurement

by Kris Hirschmann

SCHOLASTIC INC.

New York   Toronto   London   Auckland   Sydney
Mexico City   New Delhi   Hong Kong   Buenos Aires

ISBN 0-439-79060-3

12 11 10 9 8 7 6 5 4 3 2 1   6 7 8 9 10/0

Designed by Rocco Melillo
Printed in the U.S.A.
First printing, September 2005

We Dig It!

Do you want to know a secret?

We dogs are great at measurement. We come in lots of shapes and sizes. We understand the difference between smaller/bigger and shorter/longer.

Judges measure us in the show ring, so we know all about inches and feet. We even know how to use rulers.

And of course we love to take walks. That teaches us all about distance. Just follow our lead!

Smaller vs. Bigger
All the Love, Half the Size

Comparing things is the easiest way to measure. You can see right away if one thing is bigger or smaller than another. This comes in handy when you want to grab the biggest bone or the biggest toy from a pile. It's also useful if you are a little dog. When you're at the park, you can head for the other pint-size pups and ignore the huge, scary ones.

Just to be safe, I'm going to stay right here with my little brothers and sisters. We're all about the same size!

Your Turn
Which dog is the smallest?
Which is the biggest?

Jack Russell Terrier

Flat-Coated
Retriever

Dachshund

Papillon

Top Dog and Underdog

The Irish Wolfhound is the tallest dog breed. This proud pooch can be as much as 34 inches tall at the shoulder. The smallest breed is the Chihuahua, which can be just 6 inches tall.

Answers: Smallest: Papillon; Biggest: Flat-Coated Retriever

Longer vs. Shorter
The Long and Short of It

Another easy type of measurement is longer versus shorter. This is like comparing big and small, but it's not exactly the same. To say whether something is long or short, you just look at its length. The overall size doesn't matter.

Is it better to be long or short? It depends. A long leash is always better than a short one. But short toenails are definitely the way to go.

Let's have a lick-off! The dog with the longest tongue wins. Yuck! Do I smell dog breath?

Your Turn

Which tongue is shortest?
Which is longest?

Cocker Spaniel

French Bulldog

Golden
Retriever

Hot Dog!

Dachshunds are sometimes called "wiener dogs" because they are long and thin, like a hot dog. A Miniature Dachshund is about the length of two regular hot dogs laid end to end.

Answers: Longest: Golden Retriever; Shortest: French Bulldog

7

Estimating Lengths and Sizes

More Info, Please

Sometimes you need more information than just "shorter" or "longer" and "bigger" or "smaller." Try to estimate lengths and sizes by comparing things. For example, maybe you buried your favorite bone about six body lengths from the house. Or maybe you need to stay one leash length away from your owner to avoid getting caught for a bath.

I'm just one ball tall right now. But when I grow up, I'm going to be about three balls tall, like my mommy.

Your Turn

Is this dog's nose about the size of the green ball, blue ball, or red ball?

How many green balls tall is this puppy? Two? Three? Four?

Puppy Pile

Five full-grown Beagles standing on one another's backs are about as tall as one human.

Answers: Blue ball; 4 green balls

9

Estimating Distance
On the Map

You need to know how to estimate distance if you want to use a map. Maps are small drawings of big areas. On a certain map, one bone might stand for 1 mile. If a road on the map is about 6 bones long, the real thing is about 6 miles long.

3 bones

1 bone

Bow-WOW! My favorite toy is over there, just across the page. It looks like these handy lines will lead me where I need to go.

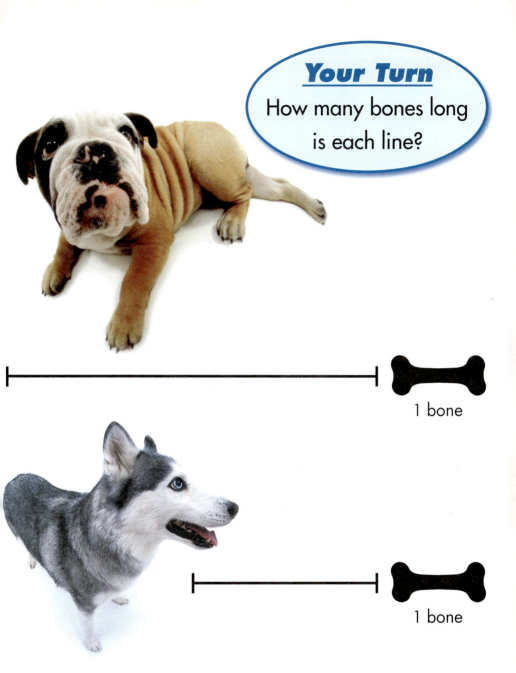

Your Turn

How many bones long is each line?

1 bone

1 bone

Mush, Mush!

In the Alaskan Iditarod race, dogs pull sleds through the snow over a 1,149-mile course. It usually takes nine days to finish the race.

Answers: 4 bones; 2 bones

11

Measuring with the Body

Is a Paw a Foot?

People were measuring things long before rulers were invented. They used their bodies as guides. An inch was the width of a person's thumb. A foot was the length of a person's foot. This system was easy to use. But it could get confusing, too, because different people were different shapes and sizes. An inch might not be the same from one person to the next.

In real life, this shoe is about a foot long. I'd wear the shoe if I could, but I'm pretty sure it's too big. In measurement terms, a paw and a foot are very different things!

Your Turn

Put your foot next to a friend's foot. Are your feet exactly the same length, or are they different?

By a Nose

Greyhounds are racing dogs. Some Greyhound races are so close that we say the winner won "by a nose." So you see, body-based measurements are still used today.

Standard Units
Keeping It Simple

Today, measurements are not based on the human body. People have invented a standard system of lengths that are always the same, no matter who is using them.

We dogs think that standard measurement units make lots of sense. With them, when two people talk about a certain length, height, or distance, they mean exactly the same thing.

What were you humans thinking?! A dog never would have invented something as silly as a unit called a tail. After all, no two tails are alike! Standard units make much more sense.

Perfect Pups

In dog-show talk, the word *standard* refers to the best pooch measurements. A perfect Boxer, for example, is between 21 and 25 inches tall at the shoulder.

What Is an Inch?
The Basic Unit

In America, the inch is the basic unit of measurement. An inch is a little bit shorter than a paper clip. It is a little bit longer than a quarter.

1 inch

This dog's nose is exactly one inch wide.
(It's nice and wet, too!)

Now that you know how big an inch is, look at the pictures on the next few pages. See if you can answer all the questions.

Your Turn

How many inches tall is this Jack Russell Terrier?

1 inch

1 inch

How many inches is this dog from ear tip to ear tip?

Now Hear This

Bloodhounds have extra-long ears. As the Bloodhound sniffs, his ears drag along the ground and stir up scents.

Answers: 4 inches; 2 inches

How many inches long is this line of West Highland White Terrier puppies?

1 inch

How many inches wide is the bucket?

1 inch

How many inches wide, from top to bottom, is this Shetland Sheepdog's open mouth?

1 inch

How many inches long is this Golden Retriever's tail?

1 inch

Give a Dog a Bone

The biggest dog biscuit ever made was 91 inches long, 21 inches wide, and 1 inch thick. Now *that's* a snack!

Answers: 5 inches; 2 inches; 2 inches; 1 inch

Using a Ruler
A New Trick

To get an exact measurement, you need a ruler. Rulers have long marks on them to show inches. Shorter marks on a ruler show parts of inches, like one-half inch and one-quarter inch.

0   1   2   3   4   5

Line up the zero of the ruler with the edge of the object you want to measure. Check the ruler to see where the *other* edge of the object ends. The lines on the ruler will tell you the length of the object.

I'm exactly 2 inches tall. My buddy stands exactly 1 inch above my head. So together, we're 3 inches tall.

Use a ruler to measure the pictures on the next few pages. See if you can answer all of the questions.

Your Turn

What is the distance from the tip of the Corgi's right ear to the tip of its nose?

Pint-Size Pup

The smallest dog in history was a Yorkshire Terrier from England. When fully grown, this dog was only 2½ inches tall and 3¾ inches long.

Answer: 4 inches

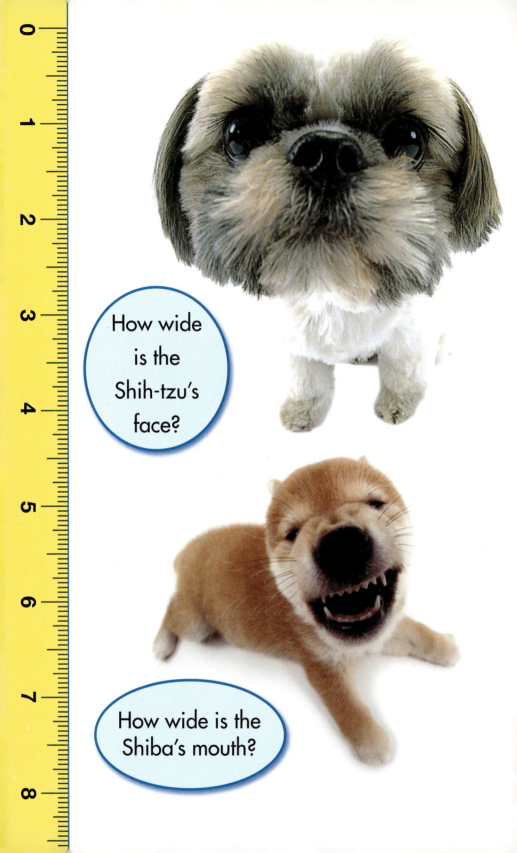

How long is the
Bloodhound's
right ear?

How long is the
Labrador's tail?

Words to Live By

There is a saying that we dogs like: "Give us an inch and
we'll take a mile." It means if you give us a little freedom,
we'll take a lot. Like maybe you want us to sit on the front
porch, but we run away down the street instead!

Answers: 3 inches; 1 inch; 2 inches; 2 inches

What Is a Foot?

The Next Step

A foot is another basic measurement unit. You can see how big a foot is if you look at the bottom of this page. If you open the book as far as it will go, these two pages together are exactly one foot wide.

A foot is equal to 12 inches. This Pug puppy is 3 inches wide. So 4 of these puppies could sit right next to one another along a foot-long ruler.

1 2 3 4 5

Your Turn

Use the ruler below to find things around the house that are about a foot long. Some of your dog's toys might be fun to measure . . . but watch out for leftover slobber!

I'm a Miniature Pinscher. In real life, I'm about a foot tall.

We Siberian Huskies are about 2 feet tall.

I've got you both beat. We Borzois are at least 2½ feet tall. (Half a foot is 6 inches, by the way.)

Massive Mutt

The longest dog ever recorded was an Old English Mastiff named Zorba. This huge dog was 8 feet, 3 inches long, from nose to tail.

| 7 | 8 | 9 | 10 | 11 | 1 |

Measuring with String
Around the Hound

Rulers are great for measuring straight lines. But sometimes you need to measure things that aren't straight. What if you need to know the distance *around* the edge of your water bowl? Rulers don't work for these kinds of measurements.

You can use string to measure odd shapes. Put the end of the string at the beginning of something you want to measure. Run the string all along or around the thing. When you reach the end of the thing, cut the string. Then measure the string with a ruler.

Use a piece of string to measure all the way around my body. But be careful, please — I'm very ticklish!

Your Turn

Use string to measure around your head, your arms, your waist, or your legs. You could also use string to measure your own dog, if he or she will let you!

Fenced In

When you measure around something, the outer edge is called the perimeter.

What Is a Yard?
Not All Yards Have Grass

What if you need to measure things that are bigger than a foot? We dogs suggest using a unit called the yard. A yard is 3 feet long. That is the same as 36 inches. To measure a yard, you could use a special long ruler called a yardstick.

In case you didn't know, I'm a Labrador Retriever. In real life, I'm about a yard long. My little puppy pals are only about a foot long. In less than a year, they'll be as big as I am!

Your Turn

How many foot-long Labrador puppies would you have to line up to equal one full-grown, yard-long Labrador?

Let's Play!

The word *yard* comes from the old Scottish word *gyard*, which means "stick." We dogs looove sticks! Do you want to play fetch?

Answer: 3 puppies

When to Use Inches, Feet, or Yards

A "Ruff" One

Now you know all about inches, feet, and yards. But do you know when to use each one?

Here's a good rule of paw:

- Use inches and half-inches for little things, like the length of your ear or the width of your nose.

- Use feet for bigger things, like the height of the fence outside your house.

- Use yards for things that include lots and lots of feet, like the distance from your house to the end of the block.

Your Turn

In real life, what units would you use to measure:

This group of Beagles? Inches, feet, or yards?

This Corgi's nose? Inches, feet, or yards?

World Record

In 1998, a dog named Taylor caught a Frisbee thrown more than 246 feet. That's the same as 2,952 inches, or 82 yards!

Answers: feet; inches

At a Glance

We're done! We've taught you everything we know. If it helps, here is a chart that compares inches, feet, and yards. Thanks for playing with us!

Love, THE DOGS

Unit	Equals
1 inch	2 half-inches
1 foot	24 half-inches
	12 inches
1 yard	72 half-inches
	36 inches
	3 feet